Lizz Murphy was born in Ireland in 1950 and emigrated to Australia in 1969 with her husband, Bill. She left school on her fifteenth birthday to work in various shops and has never looked back – she's too afraid to! From retail Lizz advanced to writing about sheep dips and bridal bouquets for a country newspaper before working as a publicist in the arts and publishing industries. She is interested in regional, community and workplace art and in using the arts to get young people excited about language. While she values the skills she learnt on the shop floor, and the family atmosphere of her first job, she's the first to encourage kids to try and stay at school and get some qualifications.

Lizz has previously published four anthologies of women's writing and two collections of poetry. She won the Anutech Poetry Prize in 1994 and was awarded the 1998 ACT Creative Arts Fellowship for Literature to develop *Two Lips Went Shopping*. She is currently the writer on *House at Work*, a book project with Parliament House, Canberra. Lizz and Bill enjoy the solitude of the New South Wales village of Binalong. They have two children, Aroona and Brendan and two grandchildren, Michaela and Georgia.

Other Books by Lizz Murphy

Everyone Needs Cleaners, Eh! (editor, TLC ACT, 1997)

Pearls and Bullets (Island Press, 1997)

Eat the Ocean (editor, Literary Mouse Press, 1997)

Wee Girls: Women Writing from an Irish Perspective (editor, Spinifex Press, 1996, reprinted 2000)

Do Fish get Seasick: A Collection of Damn Bus Poems (Polonius Press, 1994)

She's a Train and She's Dangerous: Women Alone in the 1990s (editor, Literary Mouse Press, 1994)

TWO LIPS WENT SHOPPING

Lizz Murphy

Spinifex Press Pty Ltd
504 Queensberry Street
North Melbourne, Vic. 3051
Australia
women@spinifexpress.com.au
http://www.spinifexpress.com.au

First published 2000 by Spinifex Press

Cover design by Deb Snibson, Modern Art Production Group
Edited by Patricia Sykes
Typeset in Korinna by Palmer Higgs Pty Ltd
Printed and bound in Australia by Australian Print Group

National Library of Australia
Cataloguing-in-publication data:
Murphy, Lizz, 1950-
Two lips went shopping.
ISBN 1 875559 20 5.

I. Murphy, Lizz. II. Title. III. Title: Two lips went shopping

A821.3

This title was published with assistance from the ACT Government through its Cultural Council.

This publication is assisted by the Australia Council, the Australian Government's arts funding and advisory body.

For my good friend and colleague
Janene Pellarin
who said write me a shopping poem.
So I did.

Acknowledgements

Some of the poems in *Two Lips Went Shopping* were previously published in the *ANU Poets Lunch Anthology, Blast, Canberra Arts Anthology 1999* (artsACT/National Library of Australia), *The Canberra Times, Everyone Needs Cleaners, Eh!* (Trades and Labour Council of the ACT), *Hobo*, and broadcast on ABC TV *Snapshot*.

Special thanks to David Adderton, Vivienne Cox, Sandra Forbes, Susan Hawthorne, Wendy King, Kathy Kituai, Robert Kituai, Aroona Murphy, Bill Murphy, Brendan Murphy, Harry Murphy, Janene Pellarin, Sarah St Vincent Welch and Bob Thompson for assistance and support or/and for sharing stories which inspired some of these poems. Thanks also to innumerous workmates, bosses, customers, shopkeepers and assistants, fellow shoppers, bargain hunters and travellers who supplied me with a shopping trolley's worth of poems.

'Buying a Future' is based on the article, 'Youth Allowance Brings Hard Times' by Jane Dargaville (*The Canberra Times* September 18, 1998), 'Full Moon' on 'Tusk Masters' by John Zubrzycki and 'The End of the Line' (*The Australian Magazine* July 18-19, 2000) and 'Single Mothers' is based on a story in *Passages Through Parenthood* edited by Anne Godfrey (Lothian Books), with thanks. Thanks also for inspiration gained from the general media and the fashion industry.

Thanks from the bottom of my shopping basket to Susan Hawthorne and Renate Klein for continuing to promote poets through the Spinifex Press publishing program, and to all Spinifex staff, editor Patricia

Sykes, typesetters Palmer Higgs Pty Ltd and designer Deb Snibson.

Thank you to the ACT Government and its Cultural Council as well as staff at artsACT, for making this collection possible through a 1998 ACT Creative Arts Fellowship (Literature).

Contents

Shopping 1
Betrayal 4
Soup Bones 5
Swinging 6
Short Sort 7
Menswear 9
Baby's Breath 12
Colour Code 16
Silent Partners 18
Bad Joke 20
Single Mother 22
Curtains 24

Two Lips Went Shopping 29
Kiss Kiss 30
Drop Dead Lips 31
Chic 32
Sharp Accessories 33
Treasure Chest 34
Just Like the Ads 35
The Price You Pay 37
The Natural Look 39
A New Season 41
Hard Sell 42
Brown Paper 43
First Day of Winter 45
Shopping for Chickens 46
Cash & Carry 48
Supermarket Serves 50
Fishwife 52

Sale 57
Breakfast Tricks 58
Better Bits 59
Monster Sale 60
Clearance 62
Hello Mrs Murphy 64
From the Householder 69
Eagle 70

All Heart 73
Made to Order 74
Blue 76
The Weight of Tomatoes 79
Scarlet 81
World Peace 82
You Are What You Eat 83
Imagination 84
Triumphs 86
Buying a Future 88
Dial Death 89
The Price of Technology 90
The Versatile Cleaner 91

Sold Out 97
The All Clear 99
Service-with-the-Lot 100
Kebabs 101
Eggs Over-Irish 102
The Heart of it 104
Going Strong 106

Running Free 108
Yepoon Takeaway 109
Yellow Rain 110
Brown Hills 111
Stocktake 112

Train Games 117
Stuck in a Siding 119
Connections 121
Look at You 123
Story Bag 125
Full Moon 127
How Much? 131

The Keeper 135

Shopping

Hessian leather plastic string swinging sack empty packed

brown black one two and three

over the elbow hanging by the knee

bouncing lugging swaying sagging bulging

Hessian leather plastic string swinging sack empty packed

Dragged by the hand through crowds

of women their coats bulging with flesh

their bags bulging with meat Messages for the week

hands sweeping patting my copper hair the bags

skimming my skull bumping my brow my face my cheek

Black bulky bags zipped

with grandmother treats Rowntree's

gums pastels chewy sugary sweet

and sweet

and sweet as

cosy laps

Old brown hide stretched inside

lined with potato dust

Half a stone of whites please

Tell your mammy the reds are in

Musty sacks hems rough looping stitches stacked
against shop walls
suspended scales
thud of spud clang of brass weight
two handles held wide helter-skelter grocery slide
Avalanche
Boiled
Mashed
In soup
In stew
On Sunday and
every other day

Dream of bag light as feather
wings on the side

Paper bags
white paper brown paper
newspaper

My father taught us how to make party hats out of newspaper
My mother made newspaper pokes to share out sweeties
My grandmother cut it up into squares to hang off a wire hook
in the toilet Upstairs in Woolworths she asked had they any ends
of lino just one wee piece for in front of the cooking range

How much would that be

The busy shopgirl looks harangued

Could you not just give it to me

an old pensioner

I *gasp*

at the cheek of it

manners being next to godliness ahead of cleanliness

I *gasp again*

her elbow in my side her mimed shush

She saved herself a shilling

A good housewife is a thrifty housewife

A fed pensioner is a cunning shopper

Betrayal

This is the shop I was going to when a boy
saw the ten shilling note said are you doing your
mammy's messages offered to do them for me so
I could still play My mother left broke for the rest
of the week This is the shop owned by Clarkie
in his shop coat the colour of tea and money
leaning on the broad wood counter dusted with
flour from plain loaves unwrapped unsliced in
conversation with one woman or another irritated
at our presence a penny's worth of butterballs
a penny's worth of bullseyes two penny chews
please Mr Clarke and my mammy said are the new
potatoes in yet This is the shop where I retold our
favourite joke F-U-C-K (pause) Tell her I love her
and my chum who had told it to me originally said
in her loudest most scandalised voice E-lizabeth!
and Clarkie agreed it was shocking for a nice wee
girl like me This is the shop where I learnt about
betrayal I also learnt about picking your audience

Soup Bones

So you're skinny as hell knock-kneed
and four feet something and you go to
the butcher's and he's in his navy and white stripe
and you're in your French roll which your mother
likes you to wear instead of your hair all over your
face and he says that's a lovely hairdo let me tell my
mother and this old sheila comes out from making
the sausages seventy-five in the shade and she agrees
and he says how old are you nine? and you go
no actually I'm fourteen and he's shit himself
at his mistake or is thinking soup bones have more
meat on them you look down at your thin shinbone
thin skin donkey knee scuff the sawdust floor and
your cheeks red as rare beef and that throw-up raw
flesh smell and you wishing you were all vegetarians

Swinging

This is the milk bar next door
to the dry cleaners where I worked
where the woman wore her dark hair
in a supposedly eloquent bun
like a loaf angled over an aloof white face
appeared through the swinging doors sporadically
beneath her to serve customers
This is the woman I told we were
debating premarital sex over lunch
who said but in Greece we all live together
for sixamonth after engagement
ensure the couple is compatible
If it not work out okay too bad
we do something else
She winked sneered at my youth
swung her hips weaved her pelvis
flirtatiously behind the ice-cream fridge
thrust her Mediterranean experience
her middle-aged sensuality
in the face of the Swinging Sixties
we were dying to burst on to
And then she said One-a-dollar thanks

Short Sort

This is the dry cleaning shop where I worked Saturday mornings and in the factory at the back the rest of the week Checking pockets sorting clothes men's trousers in that bin light ones dark ones suit coats in this bin woollens in another one blouses and skirts there Test all the buttons remove them if they might melt Women's dressing gowns and that smell of milk Men's overalls in a stinking heap wouldn't know where they've been until Friday last load for the week Valuables and notes dutifully returned in small envelopes amazing what they'll miss loose change in the tip boxes The hiss and steam song of the presses one for trouser legs another for the tops front creases skilfully joined The dance of the pressers from rack to press Foot pedals for steam press lock unlock from press to inspection point and the rush of metal hangers on rails for another sorting this rail to that rail according to ticket colour whisked away to all ends of the region and the women on the ironing boards and Singer sewing machines and cranky old Sid in his big sweating belly and rough old shorts swinging from pleats on the skirt press to suit coats on the dummy Pull a lever and it's a blow up doll creased sleeves or rolled Several garments on the go at once like a production line torture chamber and the spotter with her airgun her blood and bone stain removal potions and expertise On the side of the building is a twenty foot delivery boy dressed like a red and yellow bellboy and on the front plate glass windows I promote special services have your spots removed in stylish script in transparent signwriting fluid dusted afterwards with gold and silver red and yellow Bus loads of people straining their necks bemused at invisible stage doodling although it was the sixties and my skirts were getting shorter

Menswear

Menswear is all greys and browns inside leg measurements slacks with cuffs without cuffs crease resistant Long thin men short stocky men and wives angry at their husbands worse than the children Flannelette pyjamas with their gaping fronts and clock patterns navy and white singlets sleeveless short sleeve long sleeve all looking the same once they pull them out of the plastic on Steelwork's pay week rummage in your understock when you don't have their size never believe you think you're lying too lazy to check too stupid to know your own stock sorted resorted fold over fold displayed every single night every hour every bloody customer restocked every morning stock take every week counting counting . . .

Counting the hours until home-time the long dull day broken by the occasional customer returning your pleasantries a mother and a man-size adolescent with a cutting humour you can bounce off cheer both of them up as they drag cheap acrylic knits over his stubborn head her purse stretching to his overnight growth you picking his size accurately with a glance at his rounding shoulders so much they will carry he puffing his chest you more interested in his broadening back suggesting colours to go with his hopeful eyes something more fashionable than his mother will select gratefulness discreetly conveyed

You go through these same steps with middle-aged spouses they puff their chests just as much blush more The old men stay at home the old wives making it their business to know the size of all their body parts glad to escape to the shops without them buy plain wool cardigans beige enough for their inutile husbands to put on their grumpy backs dark enough to conceal the stains their nicotine fingers fumbling with fine bone buttons in neat knitted pockets searching for coins glad of a match or a spare Tallyho paper

European men shop for their own clothes the women at home cooking or still in their own country They come alone or in twos and threes loud exchanges over quality over prices Plonking their bundles their full string bags on the counters on the merchandise they dangle trousers upside down at arm's length a leg-end clutched in each hand close together then one sudden movement arms fully outstretched chin jutting at trouser crotch An instant fitting based on the theory that legs are the same length as open arms finger tip to finger tip I scan them at ground level their theory appears substantiated

My Italian supervisor tells me which nationalities carry string bags have flat heads or square jaws allow their women to come out allow them to walk by their side make them carry all the parcels About her older sisters simmering sauce all day long for the evening's pasta I learn a great deal working in Menswear I also earn more We haven't won equal pay yet but I get eight extra dollars in my pay packet for working in a traditional male retail area On my first day in this job the manager said begrudgingly he insisted on eight extra dollars worth of work He sits at a small desk in the middle of the stairwell watches the girls in their short uniforms on the shop floor keeps an eye on us as we go up and down to the stockroom I think he gets his money's worth

Baby's Breath

Lola is Italian and teaches me Italian words
We've been friends since she discovered
I could pronounce her last name properly
She gets very upset with Australians
who just can't get it don't even try
Lola's mother died when she was thirteen
They'd been living in Australia for a couple
of years when it happened
She says her older sisters were angry
with her for not wearing black
If you're Italian it's tradition to wear black
for years after someone dies
No way she said a young child in black
Anyway we're in Australia now she told them

When she told me this
she was in a black top a black cardigan
black skirt and shoes
So was I
We work in a shop and it's required dress
Our uniform
We're both annoyed with the tax department
because they won't let shop assistants claim
a uniform allowance for black shop clothes

They say they're ordinary clothes
that you can wear outside work
They must be joking
nobody would be seen dead in gear
like this unless of course you're an Italian
whose mother died fifty years ago

I'm a bit slow on other people's traditions
The other day a man and woman came in
with their son he's about nine or ten
She was wearing a black jumper
and skirt both too tight for her
She was a bit on the plump side
but they like that at least that's what
the Greek man in the cafe says
You're too thin he always says to me
and so I am but I can't help it I don't diet
or anything all the family's the same
We Greek men like something to hold on to
he says winking and his wife smiling at him
from over the chips she's frying
lapping it up or hoping to get one that night
So this Italian woman is trying on
a simple black dress with a lacey overlay
Dressy but bargain priced

I never thought anything of it
because of course whoever died
might have died a long time ago
I admired the flowers the boy was holding
An enormous bunch of small red roses
white blossoms Baby's Breath they call them
and lots of greenery ferns and things
They were beautiful expensive
The woman is struggling into the dress
in front of the mirror I'm trying to help her
and so is her husband
He seems sympathetic doesn't say much
and she doesn't speak much English
The boy interprets for them
Some people hate that they think it's bull
that foreigners come here
and don't learn the language
Soon work the *money* out they say
I think it would be very hard
Some people hate that the children
do the talking for them they say it's not right
I think it would be a big responsibility
I admire them for it
Imagine speaking two languages at that age
At any age

I step back for a minute
draw the fitting room curtain over
and let them get on with it
I smile at the boy and ask
who the lovely flowers are for
He looks at me with his big eyes
I wonder if he's translating in his head
from his own language finding the right words
It is for our dead baby he says
in a quiet precise voice
We are going to look at the grave
I didn't know what to say
I sold them the black dress though

Colour Code

This is the shop where garments hang on racks meticulously sized and colour coded where one sales assistant says that woman is no ten or twelve asks if she's checked her rear lately and the first manager on a diet of steamed chicken says you wouldn't have liked me before I lost weight I was always looking at myself in the mirror straightens her jumper yet again smooths her brown skirt yet again strains to see her wide hips pulls a face at her reflection This is the shop where finally I get to fix the fitting room curtains balancing on a chair replacing the small brass rings not for customer privacy but because the big boss is coming from head office Where customers are refused access to toilets and one says my son can just piss all over your floor then Where an elderly woman asks about discounts and the new manager crabby and of double income family status says pensioners have enough handed to them without ten per cent from us Later her sprawling new home built on a reclaimed creek bed split its sides and so did I laughing walls like white shirt linen turned to brown polyester flood mud

This is the shop where a senior assistant bent her head in fury when three women came in to browse eventually asks curtly are you right dears Turns to me and says they were our servants when we lived in South Africa stares at the backs of their black legs as they take their leave her eyes narrow as darts fingers fumbling with dress hangers and buttons and tables that have turned This is the shop where I was employed because I smiled so much and soon found it hard to smile at all

Silent Partners

1.

This is Raymonde's The girls like him They think he's a good boss and a good businessman It's a fashion shop a boutique really with the latest clothes and the plush velvet furniture up the back with the shoes You can't get shoes like this anywhere else in this town I bought a pair myself Russet suede Wedge heel And trousers almost the same colour Rust crepe straight legs cuffs I love cuffs We get everything at cost price He is a good boss Not like his wife None of the girls like her Always in a mood face like thunder Comes in pick pick pick pick Thinks because she's his wife she owns the place She's just a silent partner Not silent enough if you ask the girls

2.

That's Raymonde The girls don't like him He used to be a good boss then he got real narky when equal pay came in Had to pay us back pay as well The envelope was packed with notes God it would be great if you could give us this much every week I said I was only joking Should have seen his face if looks could kill I was dead alright It's not like I wasn't worth it We're the best staff you can get here Turns out he's been up to monkey business got found out The girls are on his wife's side Imagine doing that to a nice woman like that they all said Always knew there was something about him Everyone says she could do a better job of the business if she got half the chance Wonder if she will They might say she's only the wife I just hope we get the same staff discounts

BAD JOKE

It must've been some joke
said the mother
spite in her eyes
parcels in her arms
her life a plumbline behind her
When I walked past the shop
you were having a great laugh
your head thrown right back
Her mothertone a bitter punchline

The adult daughter
wears a portrait of herself
pinned to her chest
Her long teen neck
is white plastic downpipe
thin right angled
Her mouth is a water outlet
gaping black with yellow teeth
Her hair is red water
her eyes lead ball bearings

When she laughs this is the image
she has of herself behind a counter
giving out small change
tongue wrapped in plumber's tape
She still allows herself to laugh
even throws her head right back
but she no longer tells the jokes
doesn't want to remember the punchline

Single Mother

In the shopping centre
is the young single mother
jeans torn hair greasy
cigarette ash in the pram
She screams at her kid
Everyone looks

Everything is fine until
you get pregnant she says
If you keep the baby
you never see the guy again
How do you know a loser
How do you know if this one's
not going to be there
when you need him
What can you do if you're
on the Pill and it still happens
At seventeen you don't know
what it's going to be like
to bring up a child she says

In the shopping centre
another young woman looks on
Almost every day she is here

She stares at all the babies
in the prams
in the big shopping malls
looking for a hint of likeness

It's only been eight weeks she says
my feelings go up and down
Everyone said I was too young
Maybe I have done the best thing
it just doesn't feel like it
at the moment
At this age you don't know
what it's going to be like
to give up a child she says

Curtains

There is the lean scent of pressed cotton
calico organdie sharkskin seersucker
polyester and tulle
Pastel shades beside gingham
candy-stripe plaid paisley
Lurex
The sales assistant twirls bolts of cloth
like a band leader's staff
from varnished shelf to smooth counter
for the silver snip and ripping tear
across its metred width
She is fast on her feet and efficient at measure
as women queue notepaper in hand
this size those inches a yard of this three of that

I select black velvet
glossy shimmery a moonless night
Impressed with my choice or the price of it
she asks what I am making with this
her face whitepinched with concentration
and care for the expense
or the fantasised finished garment
I think of the part-timer where I worked
her waxen face saying I'd suit black

me screwing my nose up
When you're older she said
That week I went to the store next door
tried on a black dress round neck set-in sleeves
Suddenly I liked black so much
I wanted to be draped in it

Curtains
I say in a tone employed to ward off the evils
of my suburban state the infliction
of an orange-vinyled green-netted streetscape
Do you know dear she says in the war
when we couldn't get fabrics
we took the curtains down from the windows
and made evening gowns out of them
Her eyes rove cheered by the reminiscence
I picture velvet-curtained moves on the dance floor

She takes her time
It's a substantial purchase
I have saved for it
She can tell
Leaning across the counter
feeding the velvet hand to hand
stretching her arms the length of the metal tape
fixed on the counter's edge

rolling clunking the bolt out with her left hand
swimming the whirls of slippery cloth
back into the centre of the counter
allowing a few extra inches just in case
The bite of the shears
the loud scrunch against wood

The two lengths are folded
wrapped
soft seal skins in brown paper
They make a large parcel
broad strips of cellotape secure it
It is placed in my arms
I feel the folds slide then settle
As I wheel away my two small children
the black curtains wedged on the hood
of the pram she says remember dear
if there's another war
they'll make a wonderful ball gown

I don't know what happened
to the black velvet curtains
So many shifts
so many years
I do know that after a while
they reminded me too much of war

Two Lips Went Shopping

Two huge lips went shopping

on a pogo stick

for a red satin handbag

coordinated in colour

with their cupid's bow

Kiss Kiss

from a lipstick ad

Kiss a mate
on her long lasting matte
cherry
cherry red lips
Kiss pure comfort
sit on my tantalising
rose
tearose red lips
Kiss supremely wearable
won't rub off
berry
berry red lips
Kiss caught red handed
your fingers on my
fire-engine
smoking hot lips
Kiss kiss

Drop Dead Lips

Sitting by the pool
two octogenarians talk about ageing
I hate the way everything sinks in
the eyes the lips
Oh the lips says the other
and the cracks and creases above them
and the way the lipstick feathers into them
And the way they get thinner and thinner
says the first
Don't you paint them on says the second
She demonstrates with her lip pencil
her lip brush
draws a line up here a line around there
Artfully fills them in
Flirts with her compact mirror says
you've still got it honey
The magazines are full of lipstick ads lipstain
lipshine highshine
There's something here for both of us
she says turning a page —
Long-Lasting Colours for Drop Dead Lips!

Chic

Under pressure from Cancer Council advertising and fair skin I shop for hats get it down to jester style or balaclava opt for simple suede with medium brim which chic as I am I refrain from turning up defeating the health and safety objective I walk through the streets feeling like I have an overcoat wrapped round my head in forty degree heat find a coffee shop take the hat off put my feet up There's your hat he says and I glance across to two old women taking tea One well made up roses in her cheeks and slides in her hair The other with a dark suede hat alarmingly like my own pulled low on her face They are discussing their options Living alone and hoping for the best for the woman in the hat or booked into the chosen retirement home for the woman in rouge waiting for a vacancy She explains you have to pay a deposit make payments The woman in the hat says what if we pay all that money out and drop dead before we get in laughs at the idea of it At another table a rabbit coloured Akubra sits under its owner's chair like a carefully positioned chamber pot The plastic lining glistens its sweaty edges dark as night-time pee

Sharp Accessories

from a magazine ad

The hues of dusk the next brilliant dawn

 if i buy your knitted suit will you tell me

 i am still young

The long range forecast

 if i wear your fresh natural tones will you

 tell me i'm never going to die

A new woman is born!

 as i don your dresses should I ask what was

 wrong with the old me?

Since I started wearing lovely lingerie

I get a lot more help in the house

 if i tart around the kitchen in tits and garters

 i might get some attention

Accessories to highlight your natural potential

 glasses to suppress my soul hats to cover my

 forbidden head choker chains on my throat

Cut loose in natural fibres that won't crush

 try my silk scarf . . . last time your fingers left

 sapphire bruises

For women who hate razors that cut

 and ruby droplets they can't show off

Treasure Chest

You wake up in the morning your breasts are on your waist you think it's natural ageing something you might drape in lace You flip through the glossies turn on the box Cosmetic surgeons one by one convince you it's a disgrace You give in to their pressure agree only they can give you a body to treasure A nick a tuck a cut a slice You wake up on the table your chest is not your own You've got a double dose of silicone Slit slip extensive wound and when your body rejects it nothing to do but get it pruned You wake up in the morning they put you back to sleep Prepped again for surgery they've realised their mistake The file says perky thirty-four and you can barely fit through the door The surgeon leans over you tools of trade at hand marketing executives PR experts day-time TV hosts from across the land Don't worry we'll get it right Just let me take another measure turn your body into our treasure

Just Like the Ads

I apply one careful layer
of fake tan rubbing in
thoroughly evenly
following instructions
carefully to Celtic
shin and skin
Several hours later
I am
Hint of Lemon Rind
I apply two not so careful
not so even layers
For six more hours
my thighs cling
The cat purrs
close
too close to my calves
purr fur purr furrrr
furrrr everywherrre
I read the label
Black Walnut Shell Extract
I check the mirror
Ah all good legs
should be
Shade of Walnut Lining

I have to show off

Look at me lithe of limb

brown as any

summer slick chick

in ads by the sea

While I'm here

I water the garden

legs wet

streaky bacon

The Price You Pay

Day 1

I walk crab-like and shopping stupored
into a woman with a basket I apologise
She admits to sneaking in from another aisle
We discuss the range of bras
too many to make a decision
Then pouncing on style brand and colour
find our sizes out of stock

In the next aisle
making secondary decisions
pondering
the woman quietly reappears
I'm just letting you know I'm here now she says
So I don't walk into you again I say
So I don't give you another fright she says
We are both scared off by the prices

Day 2

I select two sports bras one grey
one white which I will wash grey
The right size for the right money

In Canberra it seems
only small-busted women play sport
In Coffs Harbour sportswomen
come in my size too
I don't actually play sport
but I don't like the implication

The Natural Look

from a bra ad

Lift mould enhance your bust bra

twist your tit off bra

push up your bust bra

tits round your ears can't hear a thing bra

enlarge by one full cup bra

milk no sugar all is sweet bra

perfect your bust profile bra

see me coming round the corner bra

smooth your silhouette bra

not a nipple in sight bra

Maximum cleavage boost and exposure bra

frostbite on the nips bra

elevate your bust bra

a climbing the corporate ladder bra

build a half-cup balconette bust bra

need a ladder to get up to it bra

extra push-up and lift bra

need muscles on your tits to get them in there bra

and for a little bit extra

if all else fails bra

or you want to go for the great divide

lose your face in there bra

the gel-filled pad that bounces like the real thing

special offer comes with free ping-pong bat bra

in all skin tones

whatever you do keep it natural bra

A New Season

It's late night shopping and
New Season Arrivals
You skim your fingers over your
heyday unexpectedly on display
your long lost fashion statements
making a comeback
arranged on hangers glass shelving
You celebrate the return
of those past eras
make a selection in quick time
eagerly climb in pull on
struggle to zip up
In the fitting room
a mirror for every angle
and you are promptly reminded
these styles are best
on one body image only and at forty-plus
you are no longer a svelte size seven

Hard Sell

The slow ending of winter dreams late morning moisture in placated trees random clumps of blossom like wet sores That faint lazy Saturday scent that dishes-in-the-sink-weekend-newspapers-cagey-book-review scent smarting-author-profile travel-pages-going-nowhere smell That urge to take action but what the hell linger-here-all-day smell Permission to let go of the news until later Save the tally of the dead and the done for until after-breakfast-settled-stomach brewed coffee smell Ignore the world in its black ink columns with that faint-but-not-quite-smoke smell burning rubber smell of the motoring pages faint-but-not-quite-earth scent of the gardening pages The rainforest this paper once grew out of saw-mill-paper-mill-newsprint aroma That remember-to-recycle-the-hard-sell smell of the advertising pages and by the way have you forgotten the tip closes at noon

Brown Paper

Anniversaries fly by
become ribbed fingers
at my breastbone
I feel your presence there
or wish for it
Doors ajar invite steps into a room
blooming in low watt bulbs
Daffodils bow their heads
The eyes of potatoes turn away
surprised to find plants grown
from their peeled skins
discarded at the bottom of the garden
the owner in shaking head
rubber gloves and spinster tartan

Laughter is a piece of crackling
Stories are coats hung on pegs
Come in close the door
switch on the light go out
when I snuff you behind the ears
leave your messages in the freezer
My pocket books are spirit and string
My life is brown paper
it heaves with meat

The butcher walking down the street
his hands unscrubbed
his beefy forearms
luminous pink globules
the raw smell hanging on like death
in broad daylight

First Day of Winter

I like the ritual of slicing chopping the scraping of ingredients from scrubbed wood board into simpering hot water its ripples reflecting shining steel the steam holding memories of other kitchens other hands at work over the sink over a bench or a turned leg table It's the first day of winter Yesterday I made the first pot of soup for the season a day early With chicken carcass and spare nobs of white meat and the gizzards if I had them I simmer barley lentils split peas Bright orange carrots are small rough hewn fireballs too eager to cut in thin even discs I slice transparent celery its hard ribs resisting my fingers shred the few remnants of ragged paper leaves wish for that deep green tone and celery earth taste that grocers throw on the refuse heap Add dark shadow parsley finely snipped and abundant Promise next time it will be home-grown Know I will break that promise Leeks The onion white root end the slices circled like rings of a tree shades of lime and opaque leaves texture of leather shape of knife blade Tough old parsnip piquant scent like the knobbled fingers of women who have filled many mouths

Shopping for Chickens

Old women white skin
left without sunshine
Light pulpy flesh
scent of kill freshness
keen as axe heads

And at home preparing
worn wood chopping board
slicing and trimming
spicing basting
Between plump legs
breadcrumbs herbs
pungent onion

And after
The cleaning
A nobule of white meat
a sliver pink tinted
translucent
Clots of rich blood

My kitchen table
is dirt-ground and flies
My kitchen knives
old blades rusting
or already blood smeared

I am old woman chicken claws
keeping young girls pure
Their fathers send them
their mothers bring them
I no longer hear the screams
as village women straddle them
hold them still their limbs apart
Or the crude cut of skin
the wrest of paltry pieces of
flesh from their child bodies
Afterwards legs lashed
for primitive healing

If I was making soup
I would truss this chicken
with coarse string
just like my grandmother
her fast hands work-moist
She never could understand
how my grandfather
hated the taste
Maybe he knew this poem
was already in my veins

CASH & CARRY

Birth Mother
what did you think
as they roped you to the table
stuffed towels in your mouth
needles in your spine
your check-up a checkout
for your child

Birth Mother
what went through your head
as they split your body
ripped your bar-coded babe
pre-term from your belly
said she was dead when you could see
her life ahead of you without you

Birth Mother
what did you think
when they left you roughly laced together
of the ache of the rich white
wouldbe mommies
in the queues at adoption hotels
dollar notes at the ready

Birth Mother
what did you think
of the agony of caesarian rape
without adequate anaesthetic
and the emptiness in your womb
in your heart sliced open
like a sample pear on a market stall

Birth Mother
what went through
    your head
        after they selected
            your child
    from the baby trade
            cash & carry

Supermarket Serves

for Wendy

At the deli section we take a number
from the ticket dispenser a hot-faced girl
runs out of humour has heard all the chicken insults
as we comment on sparrow size
and one bird still giving up the ghost
neck skewed wings flailing
Strands of hair fall across her face
as she repeatedly stabs one chicken
finally securing a proper hold
with serving fork then struggling with foil bags
Her first day serving in a shop harder than she dreamed
and she isn't going to be nice to this old chook
Over the Easy-Lite Ham a blonde woman
weighs thinly sliced meat is pleasant
The girl summoned leaves sullenly
pulling long hairpins from her dull head

In the baking aisle we are choosing
one-minute bread mixes
A knowing customer stops in our tracks
Oh the bread is so beautiful she says
The potato and herb very herbie she says
so cheap she says calculating

Magnified by thick glasses her eyes stare large blue pools
at the shelves head waving in affirmation
You'll really like it she says
continues on her way pauses shouts back
Good luck with the bread
At the fish counter Atlantic trout lies sliced in ice
beside prawns high priced in seablue ticket writing
And earlier at the pet porpoise show
the only Antarctic Leopard Seal on Australian land
bounds out to bask on paddling pool plastic
Perform for silver titbits

FISHWIFE

In my ocean dreams
I swim the silk sea
the blue lilac deep

I am the dolphin
arcing horizons
finning bright skies

I am pearl teeth
smile-diving
in skirts of red weed

I am the mullet run
skirting the shore
in a silver flash

I am translucent jelly
tentacle trailing
I am tumbling sponge water

I am salt

On my holidays
incognito
in my asphalt tourist shorts

I visit markets by the first light
meet with the fish
warn the bluefin tuna

Listen for the sashimi auction
listen for the three second dollardrop
listen for your last raw cut

I am the catch of the day
haul me in on my shell coaster
dine from my clam dish

I am the fishwife
ocean starers view my estuary
from the giftshop marine treasury

Sale

SALE

SALE

SALE

The banner sways

above the heads

of gliding shoppers

still and straight

as statues

down escalators

One knee bent

up escalators

shop window

mannequins

going cheap

on a wet Monday

BREAKFAST TRICKS

It's early Before business hours and the cafe is packed with workers putting off the inevitable Policy makers and business people are already at it networking and bargaining over dim tables coffee and croissants There is a flow of food and conversation Phrases fragments of fermenting deals drift in my direction Two men lean in to each other one inspired thumping his cup in its saucer knows every trick in the book The other uneasy rattled They are marrying up invoices They are setting someone up Someone with a woman walking him through the mountains Feeding him up They wonder how he got through life this far agree he should be wearing a napkin that he must think they both fell out of a tree There are things to be said without saying them Lips purse instead Heads shake shoulders stiffen Now tell me this says one do you The other knows what's being asked says not for twenty years no no There is thigh slapping coffee draining The confident man is conspiratorial the security you know that's all I wanted today The other is thin-nosed visibly relieved at this clear understanding

Better Bits

At the recycling centre men pick over old timber
and mower parts Kids check out rows of bicycles
Washing machines and fridges rust in the open air
One woman has bought large cement pavers
The front of her P-plated car noses the air as she lifts
the heavy round weights into the boot one by one
In Scottish overtones as short and clipped as her
physical self she explains she will put them across
her lawn He warns her the steering will be light

Inside the shed labelled Better Bits shelves are
stocked with green and brown bottles broken lamps
tinny radios cheap cups and plates Shop dummies
spoon each another in a corner their broken arms
exclamation marks their permanent blue irises stark
stops constantly observing rummaging bent heads

At the Binalong tip we dispose of our rubbish pledge
again to compost or buy a few chickens Make way
for resident ibis white feathers dusted grey as ash
heads black as garbage bags eyes glistening plastic
No mannequins here just the bent tin of old farm
sheds and the shells of wrecked cars the holes for
headlights gnawing your back like more staring eyes

Monster Sale

Under the 'Auction at 2pm' sign
they exchange symptoms
arthritic ravages
She needs a knuckle replacement
holds her hand out flat
finger bones curving in all directions
like swerving tines on silver serving forks
He slowly raises a sleeve
his elbow a billiard ball
winces as he slides the shirt down again

We say we could raise more funds
if we auctioned spare body parts
knee joints elbow joints knuckle bones
That's nothing to laugh at he says
braces straining over red flannelette
When the Monster Garage Sale is over
stalls packed trundled off raffles drawn
antique desks and sundry items
cheap under the hammer
I stop at the shop to buy pasta

Vermicelli Fettucini

Penne Linguini

Little Hat/Cappelletti

Bow-Ties or Spaghetti

Little Ears/Orrecchiette

Shells and Elbows

Brittle as old bone

CLEARANCE

for Aroona and Brendan

At the clearance sale we are successful in our bidding Eight dollars for sixteen pigeons all grey but one brown and white beauty Standing room only in makeshift rolled wire netting cages Our children are wide mouthed pleased with the acquisition A small boy is puff-faced with disappointment It is agreed that we will share Money changes in adult hands Eight pigeons each and we keep the brown one They remind us of the city and our own childhoods always neighbours with pigeons That soft coo flap of wings rap of seed tin in the twilight Birds arriving from everywhere to settle under rough wood and wire on top of a shed roof Big brothers or fathers climbing ladders to bring them in watch they don't shite on you but you know it's good luck Pigeons like heights and after a week or two when it is safe to let them loose ours take to the roof cooing across the hills Wish we had their view Later and more adventurous we drive them to the next village to demonstrate how pigeons find their own way home Every day after school the children check the roof for a line of soft grey birds and one brown Several kilometres away a pigeon fancier's flock has swelled while our water collected from the tin roof is running clear The children don't think this is a fair trade at all

HELLO MRS MURPHY

1.

Hello?

Hello

Mrs Murphy?

Yes

Hello

LookfirstofallMrsMurphythankyousomuchfor supportingus [my favourite charity] *lasttimeitwasverygenerousofyouwe're wonderingifyouwouldliketosupportusagainwith anotherpurchaseofcardsforeveryoccasion they'redifferentdesignstolasttime*
[she hastens to add] *socanIputyoudownfor anotherorderMrsMurphy?*

Hello?

Mrs Murphy?

Mrs Murphy's recall is sifting through last time's order no-one she can think of who would want the dated designs the draped strings of pearls dainty dintzy china teacups

dingy straw hats daisy lazy floral patterns
Veiled merged and muted still lifes you could
only send to someone visually impaired They
protrude from the top drawer take up space

Mrs Murphy?

Um no.

2.

Hello?

Hello

Mrs Murphy?

Yes

Hello

AhMrsMurphyI'mringingfromPayasYouView TV?

But . . .

I paid last month's . . .

[guilty conscience] . . .

Wewerejustwonderingifwecouldinterestyouin installingViewTV?

Hello?

Mrs Murphy?

We already have it . . .

[do your research] . . .

Ohwellahhisthereanyoneelsearoundyourway

who mightbeinterestedthatyoucouldputusonto?

Hello!

Mrs Murphy!

3.

Hello?

Hello

Mrs Murphy?

Yes

Hello

OhMrsMurphyI'mringingfromACladtobeHad

FactoryuphereinSydneyandIwaswonderingif

you couldtellmewhatyourhomeismadeof?

Hello?

Mrs Murphy?

Mrs Murphy's recall is sifting through all the materials a house might be built from So many Double brick brick veneer mud brick pisé maybe stone cypress fibro weatherboard even tin if you're unlucky Slabs and bark if you're a pioneer settler Something there rang a bell Doorbell Can't come now I'm on the phone I'm always on the phone speaking to fairy floss voices . . . how long have I been on the phone . . . long enough not to remember . . .

Um

Could you hold on please?

YesthankyouMrsMurphy

Um

Fibro
[I just checked]

YesthankyouMrsMurphynowMrs Murphy
couldIinterestyouinaluminiumcladdingtomake
yourhomelookbrightandnewwecansend
someonetogiveyouanestimateanditwillonlytakea
fewlifetimestopayoffanyhow?

Hello?

Mrs Murphy?

Hello?

Mrs Murphy?

Mrs Murphy!

Mrs Murphy leaves the line dangling slowly unwinds herself from the sugarpink cocoon sifts through brochures for a different sales pitch one one that might get her off the caught-working-from-home-telemarketing hook Mrs Murphy picks up the receiver again

Hallo?

Do you sell answering machines?

From the Householder

Leafing through
mail order catalogue
I am inspired by
Chinese love poem sheet sets
write pillow talk
feathers of discourse
suggesting intercourse
seal my ditty
in the return address envelope
of my lips
sign it
from the householder
leave it on the bedside table
of my hips
say drop a line
if you like my sales pitch

EAGLE

The phone rings right
in the middle of Tai Chi
on pay TV

You rang right in the middle
of Eagle Grabs its Prey
I say
and now the eagle goes hungry
prey long gone
but it's okay
I'm not into blood sports anyway

All Heart

for Sarah

Write about the contents of my bag she said Interview me she said I remember this friend of mine in early morning meetings fumbling over cappuccinos her hands lost deep in the bottom of a violet striped backpack remnants of her travels leftover life plans office scraps and strings of prose unravelling like intricate knitting and eventually the gold and silver coins like perfect words picked and plucked for exact tone and tenor her story sung over cooling coffee Now in need to distribute weight her trouser pockets swell with keys and necessities She carries one tiny pouch threaded under arm over head a square of high polished leather It sits on the front of her body all heart

Made to Order

It's the last day of the year I trudge through nostalgia visit a former home perch on a new fountain stretch my legs over terracotta pavers arch my feet at ageing shop facades a coat of many colours prosaic tiles a mozaic of decor and era linked by an exuberance of modernity Blue gateways archways high glass ceilings closing in part of the original street water sculptures pot plants and tall palms A summer breeze from the ocean as if made to order I think of a bad painting a watercolour with all the stumbles exposed the light blotted out with graphite scumbles the translucency rubbed till the Ingres paper sheds layers in dirty particles It's busy with post-Christmas sales or pay week Children play in the sandpit shoppers dip hands in flowing water (not enough public toilets the old people said) rest bags on decorative brick walls Two women straighten pat tight garish cardigans black scarves folded across foreheads accentuating smiles outlining laughter Teacups clink on a balcony This is where I had my driving lessons the instructor telling me to slow down for the madness pedestrians wandering over the road like they owned it and now they do I walk both sides of the familiar slope Some of the shops have been here forever the plumber with his dusty display area empty but for a sink and toilet propped against the wall Stood in front of it many times when a bus stop was here wished he sold televisions left one on for us The hotels have renovated their interiors upgraded their image holiday-makers sipping wine and beer outside in the sun bands playing loudly inside in the dark At this end the shops peeter out just a pawn shop the fruit shop with its 'New Australian' family still putting in long hours and an openness that suggests the beach is not far away As young mothers we pushed our prams along here loaded up with nappies and bottles Finally tired of window shopping we took to gazing at white sand and the endless sea

Blue

The stage is blue Mostly blue

You can run your hand through the blue light

smell the varnish of the now blue kitchen chair

read the cues placed there

A day-sky backdrop shines out to where later

there will be indigo darkness

Indigo magic

Katerina's mother sits in the blue light of her kitchen There is a scattering of scissors sliced newsprint She reads over the letter she has just written smooths the creased newspaper articles flattens the fold through the long column crumples what is left of the flapping page into a ball piles the fine paper trimmings straightening the edges She pushes them together like nail clippings but instead of finger-tipping them up and into the kitchen-tidy she pats them almost as if attaching them to the polished table their backs already glued

She writes her daughter in Sydney often She is good daughter and she misses her but she is happy for her Her new life new friends She has her career now Her father has bought house and put her in it Katerina can pay rent or pay back better than loan with bank Give her start

That shoe shop hard work Long days and the girls never stay All those hard cardboard boxes brown grey white lids like sharp words from the men standing in the back Looking over shoulder proud to be boss Too proud to do work Rustling tissue paper around shoe after shoe Sickening synthetic smells remind me of childbirth and the first time we did it I told Katerina it wasn't so good Katerina worried too much she was missing something She found out Bled everywhere she say Is nice we can tell each other But not in front of her father

Short Greek men Their men friends Their card games Their politics Their short stubborn dicks with no love cold hands grappling your flesh your fat they like your fat I hope you eat up Katerina Too thin if want Greek boy Is cooking for herself now she buy microwave oven

Dear Katerina

I have found good Greek recipes for new microwave oven and cut out for you Also AIDS I hope you like these stories . . .

Love

Your Mum

The Weight of Tomatoes

It's a late opening supermarket
with bright lighting quiet floors
wide white freezers
rows and rows of European foods
and fishes labels in foreign tongues
jars of preserves legumes in brine
small ripe bulbs in coloured juices
We are on the way home
from talks of peace
pictures of war
We carry images of dead children
smoking bodies
blood like a growing beetroot stain
seek solace in soft green avocadoes
choose rose red tomatoes
A young guy in a jacket scarlet
as tomato skin prints out weight
and price on red and white stickers
You're not your usual self we say
Edges crumple as he smooths
tacky paper around one firm fruit
folds his arms tells us yesterday
his best friend died shares the details
He remembers the things they did

the good times they had
While he's working he says
he doesn't think about it so much
We offer condolences feel the weight
of ripe tomatoes heavy in our hands

Scarlet

Scarlet as bird bones
I walk through infant laughter
and colour-splashed smiles
Sip on coffee and postcard images
children with missing limbs
Ask when will the landmines
know the war is over
Enter into the intimacies
of other cafe goers framed
in small brown windows
Watch their eyes become split
flesh scarlet then turquoise birds
delicate wings broken

World Peace

We watch the progress of peace talks Hold our breath for news that will hold our people together Hold our breath for news in fear that the next killing will be our own We watch the progress of other wars Hold our breath for news of bigger threats Hold our breath in fear for the people of the world Watch the madding crowds fight for their futures fight for basic rights fight back for what they believe in An Australian airline promotes world peace A white dove frozen in flight on a magazine page of indigo night Peace as commodity Travellers whisked away relax safe in the knowledge that this airline will continue the quest Two hundred airport lounges and complimentary snacks

You Are What You Eat

with thanks to David

He eats green and lean and things called nutolene and stuff made from soya bean and harvests straight from the fields in packets in shadowy jades brands that sound sun blessed and sanitised Golden labels emboldened with words like abundant and earth and even easy cooking Ingredients like bird seed — oatflakes chickpeas and falafel mix Legumes and those just add water vegieburger turns We buy them to try them to break the cycle of dripping red meats dead weight animal treats segmented with axes saw-toothed knives and scissor blades After all you are what you eat But somehow on those last bare cupboard days before pay days and shopping days we go to the pantry licking our canines and all that is left are those chartreuse health food lines those vegetarian plates edging ever closer to their use-by-dates

IMAGINATION

Imagination is
corners of flesh
white skin
a darting eye
a smile a grimace
fingers splayed
around books
for author signing
clutching
purses wallets
red leather bags
black patent
silver quilted
tangerine weave
straw hat to match
backpacks in every
colour fabric
suede pigskin
a haversack
black quotation
on pocket flaps
slung casually
across a young
T-shirted back

one strap slipping

like an evening wrap

teasing

read my verse

Imagination is . . .

TRIUMPHS

You really want to read him but then
he dies in the telling says a young book lover
over afternoon tea
In the coffee queue a golfer practices his strokes
catches a pube or more in his underwear
unashamedly achieves relief finger and thumb
gripping the edge of white trouser crotch
legs astride knees eased
Behind the glass par-cooked battered fillets
are like soles of feet
or my tough baked potato skin
the salsa corn blended avocado shredded cheese
sour cream and shallots a triumph in balance
And then the toy-size plastic cutlery
This rackety feeding centre for shoppers
voices rising bells ringing skunk-style haircuts
and the pressure to play it black and blonde cool
What's your last name
His question follows the bend of the servery
She tells him issues it like a challenge
her laugh a striped coat as she leaves
crumbs sweep to the floor
as he returns to his floor-mopping

Buying a Future

They give us this youth allowance
and if you saw the ads you'd think it was better
but it's means tested on my mum's income
I couldn't afford to live in
my own place on Newstart
and now I get even less
because Mum works
and now I have to live with Mum forever
Mum's a saleswoman
it's not like she's rich
and now I can't even give her board
so she's worse off
and I get less than half I used to
so I'm worse off
$68 a fortnight hardly covers
my bus passes and I need them
for chasing jobs
and they said I had to have a mobile phone
so I got one
Now I can't afford it
I have to look smart for interviews
but I can't buy any clothes
Now they say they're concerned
about youth suicide

They want us to be more optimistic
about the future
They're asking what tools do we need
Money's the only thing I need
Give me a decent dole
so I can pay for my bloody mobile
buy my interview clothes
and get a job
earn my own money
buy myself a future
Let's see them put that in an ad!

DIAL DEATH

Keep the city clean
Don't let them score

Keep it crime free
Don't let them score

Remove the planters
so they can't hide the score

Remove the seats
so they can't sit as they score

Remove the phone booths
so they can't shelter as they score

Now they're out in the open
Standing Scoring

Dealing
With death on a mobile

The Price of Technology

At the community kiosk a volunteer perches on a stool supervises the arrival of small green shoots struck in plastic pots tin cans Her co-worker arranges prices roughly written on pieces of card-board Racks of second-hand garments grey as the men gathering nearby for the kiosk opposite a public toilet the height of modern technology automatic doors automatic washing-out efficient Men standing in groups on the pavement waiting their quiet turn waiting for the wide door slide bathroom interior flashing passersby seat up every time Not half as efficient as the six at a time urinal

The Versatile Cleaner

From the Product Data Bulletin —

Colour: Royal Blue/NiceEmulsification: Excellent

Flash point: None/Where's the flasher?

Foam: Medium/At the mouth?

Cost effective/Cleaning women cheap

Safe on all surfaces/Except skin hands and eyes

Penetrates into normally inaccessible surfaces/Every crevice of your body

Rinses freely leaves a shine

Takes water scale light rust/Takes your health

Safe on all metals/Cleaners are not robots

Safe/if not swallowed not splashed in the eye not spilt on the skin

Dilute Seek medical assistance Irrigate for fifteen minutes

Seek medical assistance if effects persist

Wash thoroughly/Comes in drums

Faint spice fragrance/A cleaning woman's perfume

For most hard surfaces/How hard is your cleaner's shiny surface?

From the Material Safety Data Sheet —

Appearance:

Clear royal blue mobile liquid

with a faint spicy fragrance

Sounds of the ocean let me put my hands in

my tongue in

my face in

Let me dive into it drown in it

safely

spicely

Let me be swept along on the tide

of this no-known-fire-hazard-from-the-product product

as I scrub the bathroom tiles

smile into porcelain breathe deep as a super clean

television advertisement

Health Hazard Information:

Can be severely irritating if swallowed

Corrosive to eyes May cause severe

and permanent damage

Can cause skin irritation and can de-fat

the skin with continual contact

Available information

indicates there is little or no hazard

when the vapours are inhaled

No hazard or little hazard?

Hazard a guess How little is little?

Hazard a guess about the unavailable information

Hazard a guess why it is unavailable

Research is expensive?

Research results are suppressible

Cleaners are disposable

First Aid for the Eye:

Irrigate with copious amounts of water

for at least fifteen minutes

Seek IMMEDIATE medical attention

Take your white stick (nearest toilet brush will do) and

SHOW THIS SAFETY DATA SHEET TO A DOCTOR

ask them to translate into Braille

Cleaners will need it in all languages

Precautions for Use:

Use in a well ventilated area

How small are the bathrooms you clean?

As the product can cause eye irritation

safety glasses or goggles must be worn

Gloves recommended for prolonged use

How many bathrooms per day do you clean?

Safe Handling:

Don't store near foodstuffs

Spillages are slippery

Absorb with dry earth

Shovel up Keep spectators away

KEEP OUT OF REACH OF CHILDREN

Put in the hands and eyes of cleaning women

Sold Out

In the centre of the small town was a department store where the good country folk met all their needs from clothes and cutlery to linen and cut glass and up the back a grocery section and best of all a charge-it facilitating home delivery and a walk-through from the houses at the back to the shops in the main street not that there were that many Then the department store gave in to profit-line pressure rationalised and the long-loyal sales women one by one powdered their cheeks and commuted to less personal chains Closing 49 were advertised stock allowed to deplete shelves emptying by the day and residents long faced on the footpath not knowing what would become of them or the town They've let us down they said The business people were in two minds a dividing line practically painted down the middle some said stuff them we managed before them we'll manage without them others having read too much bush poetry swore we'd all be ruined In this regard the newsagent was animatedly adamant For him after the rural crisis and then the recession this was the last straw immediately spending money for fear of losing it A coat of paint a new awning we knew he would get out soon as he could sell out The local rag did its bit interviewed the shoppers at the depth of their depression recorded stirring words for and against sent down the most inciting news since Farmer Brown's cows pointed the finger straight at the chain owners after all as one shop owner said they'd left us there like a bird on the outside of a bikkie tin As the last of the staff painted the windows white pasted closed stickers over the closing sale posters the phone call came not like the movies where it's in time to save you from death row but the newspaper head office to say you can't go saying things against major advertisers Eventually someone purchased the empty premises turned it into an arcade for small retail outlets the town didn't have the trade to support Tried everything in it And now as we walk past the latest closing down/all stock must go sign community opinion has never been more united Sold out alright!

The All Clear

A series of white concrete drains
perforate the landscape like the edge
of spiral bound paper brushing blueness
combed with fine cloud and the breath
of angels Wheat stubble is a lavender lake
brown horses gather in woolly winter coats
three men wear gold turbans luminous as
candles and canola crops and a teenage girl
stares out from under angry eyelids as we
park in front of the cafe where painted roses
look like big flat onion halves Youths in
lalloping limbs droopy young-men-faces carry
takeaways scratch dicks Temora is a town
of clear conscience low white facades
long skies Sunday window shopping and
a butcher shop sign that promises: No Dogs

Service-with-the-Lot

Our orders for hamburgers-with-the-lot
are taken without smiles or thank yous
We talk about the shock of poor service
dour faces rudeness
How no-one seemed to have any idea
We talk of the improvements over the years
tourist and hospitality training
differences it has made
Our overseas guest is surprised would never
have expected from these warm people
Everyone is so friendly say the visitors
the celebrities who have come here before him
famous faces on the media promoting us down-under
Our hamburgers arrive are slapped on the table
The coffees don't come at all
We're still waiting for service-with-the-lot

Kebabs

A tidal wave of yellow green
then pink foliage Along the road
gnarly gums with clumps of yellowing
mistletoe like shoppers swinging with
distended plastic bags and a Clydesdale
distinctive white smear up his ribs
on his nose In Tumut a cafe lawn of galahs
consuming seeds Some still threaded overhead
like kebabs on thin deciduous spokes

Eggs Over-Irish

for Harry

At our Armidale stop where the waitress
is efficient and delightful a well thatched man
saunters through the kitchen area on muscled
calves narrow ankles Popping grapes into his mouth
he checks unnecessarily that we are being served
as his wife works swiftly serving coffees filling trays
Are you timber-cutters he asks The beards he says
Quickly I check my chin my upper lip realise almost
gratefully I am not being acknowledged at all
For as long as it takes to cook our Shearer's Breakfasts he talks
What about everyone fighting each other in Ireland he says
You would know I say I am brave when I am invisible
and in the company of two Irishmen burly as timber-cutters
Armidale is so green the nearest thing to Ireland he says
Why do they call it New England I say
And deciduous trees all around the region
We are native lovers I say
How there is no crime only the Aboriginal community
always breaking in to a few shops he says
White-fellas never steal I say
When you go to Tamworth put your hand out
the car window it will be ten degrees hotter he says
She didn't do the eggs over-Irish he says I'll tell her he says

The trouble with small places like yours he says
is if you fall out with the baker you don't get your bread
As we're leaving he's returning to the cafe with a sliced loaf
We wonder which village like ours finally ran him out of town

The Heart of it

Billboards shout warnings
from the towns ahead
In Tamworth there are 50,000 of us
just thought we'd tell you in case
you were thinking of starting any trouble
And the slogans
Keep it in mind
says a defeatist Lake Keepit
as if assuming nobody
would ever really stop there

Tamworth is
the heart of the country
and it's the annual country music bash
We've heard that thousands attend
that there is music on the streets
in shop doorways everywhere you go
A muso told us they go all night
In the end you just want to tell everyone
to shut up and then when you're trying
to get some sleep and some yodeller
sets up under your hotel window

Solo singers appear
on stage by the river
there are marquees
cowboy hats a few cars
just a sprinkling of an audience
Perhaps it's because it's day time
or maybe the event is not in full swing
most people in normal daily routines
or just passing through like ourselves
keeping it in mind for next time
but always passing through
looking from the outside never really
getting to the heart of things

Going Strong

Molong is 150 years old
and still going strong
if you believe the tourist signs
In this street number ninety is
blackening boards horizontal aged
A woman venerable in blue dress
stretches her geranium pink arms
a warm horizon
across the walk of her verandah

Number ninety-one is swathed
in flesh coloured blooms
bunches hang off windowsills
A silver birch drops
spider string branches
Its leaves are paper ribbons
twisted on the end of kite tails
olive as ancient hills
against a slim powdery stem

Another garden boasts
a spear-carrying statue black as coal
loin cloth and beard white as snow
If his concrete lips could move
what would he say
minimum 40,000 years
and like the stereotype
still going strong

Running Free

Emus brilliant blue on black heads
and necks run free in feather skirts
Blood orange plains followed by verges
littered yellow koala and kangaroo traffic signs
escaped sunflowers basking broad gold crowns

It feels wet coastal The hotel is basic
Downstairs pleasant Friendly enough
Upstairs the sheets are crisp
No comment on the bedspread curtains torn
furniture stark walls unwashed
I avert my eyes from a vertical-stained corner
look forward to that drink

At 5 am someone pisses from a nearby window
the irritating convenience of male anatomy
Street machines Orange lights sweeping a wake-up call
Yesterday I couldn't place Gunnedah although
I know we've been this way palm trees jacarandas
brash green fronds not in my memory
Now they are painted images along with the old
Airflow fan worth knocking off if we were dishonest
A bit off-centre in early heat sounds just like
someone urinating on an iron roof

Yeppoon Takeaway

The edge of the continent chewed like finger nails
is all energy A snow storm of free-falling seagulls
surfers appearing on a broken sea surface and cold-
armed women warming their chests across the road
on white-paper-parcel fish and chips

Street lights switch on are amber moons
the deep sea turning to dark ink fusing with evening
and shadows The surfers vanish Given up on the
whitewater froth or coasting in on hunger pangs and
ocean food smells Even eagles bronze winged black
tipped look for takeaways

Yellow Rain

At the Big Banana adults freely irrisistibly
pick up squeeze squeak while signs
forbid children to touch There are Big Banana
cups key rings serviette holders beer coolers
tooth pick holders stress bananas cushion bananas
banana ornaments It is raining bananas
A woman in a wheelchair says I get drunk
and fall down I'm thinking party animal then realise
she's reading comic signs aloud I share this with her
and she thinks it's a great joke
Her partner joins in says how do you think
she ended up in a wheelchair
A tour of the plantation has just come to an end
A burst of senior citizens women in red sequinned
jumpers others laughing
Tourists buy souvenirs in bundles select postcards
We buy a bag of real bananas for a dollar
complain because the toboggan rides open daily are closed
Nearby a township protests at aerial spraying
while children travel to and from school
the local paper photographs them at the bus stop
They wear raincoats the colour of bananas

Brown Hills

for Vivienne

On a brown hill
a mother with low income
and lackadaisy husband
stands with her two thin girls
gawk-eyed at the window of their home
as the large department store blazes
flames casting strange light across the city
Razed to the ground the building
the merchandise the lay-bys the records
And in the fire the mother's account
all her white goods the fridge
the freezer a twin-tub washing machine
another seven years of slow scraping debt
An honest woman she died ashamed
that she never wrote and told them
how much she owed them

STOCKTAKE

from the media 27 December 1997

Department store chains battle it out for every last consumer dollar what's left of it after Christmas spending Their broadsheet advertisements like red and white flags luring sale shoppers in There's no other place to be today and they believe it line up early morning at store doors plastic cards creaking wait big eyed and beyond their means for everything to be slashed No wonder Australian donations are on a slowdown though drought crisis persists in PNG hundreds of thousands in extreme danger and children dying In Jakarta drought delays harvests the factories are closing the economy collapsing the people so poor they huddle homeless in the streets Or are so rich they can pay more than a factory worker's wage on one Ecstasy night out In Algeria the headcount reveals only two seats out of nearly a hundred for a movement towards a peaceful society and ninety civilians massacred In the hamlet of Shari twenty-eight throats slashed bodies hacked to pieces one man eighty-eight years old five women fourteen children one baby six months In Sidi el Antar the count is up to fifty-three throats slashed bodies hacked mostly women mostly children In Algiers four children four women three men In London all is well now that women in the forces will shoot to kill but back in Australia there is unfolding disaster as Melbourne's casino-promises of jobs for ordinary people sit on shaky ground Like the ads say it's time to stocktake

Train Games

Stuck behind a mechanically deficient freight train we wait for it to pull in let us overtake pick up time A restless young man sits beside a man playing Solitaire Do you mind if I join you he says The other man is soft accented Sure he says The young man is so nice overnice wants more than a place to sit I watch his profile flick between the seats in front of us the older man's shining scalp reflected in the darkening window They play several games of cards The young man brings chilled water says one more game for the road He is studying film got word his mother is unwell taken a week off After a rest the older man speaks freely His voice merging with the murmer of wheels on clacking tracks He speaks of bombs and destruction is animated in night black glass The young man's bottom-lip greed for a story swells ruby So you want to go home? The older man's hair is scant but his right ear is voluptuous Do I want to go home of course! But I have no choice he says I am jealous of this red young mouth which has licked out the scent of this man's loss Everyone plays cards on train journeys I have forgotten how The Queen's Slipper pack we bought for two bucks in the buffet car sits unused On someone else's tray is a gilt lettered bible with funereal black ribbon marker Earlier this woman talked eagerly to passengers asked them to complete questionnaires Nora Joyce's biography has given me a taste for scandal and other people's stories too I thought the train would be filled with holiday-makers tourists but these are carriages trucking people who just have to be some place else The train is agitated Its sound muffles quiet talk of religious theories spirituality souls and end of life goals What a life says the older man The young one excuses himself goes off to write a script make a movie about it some day

Stuck in a Siding

Stuck in a siding with a homes and garden magazine a young thin mother with infinite patience and remaining happy two year old twins an elderly woman who says nicely only babies need dummies and another getting frustrated with pocket Nintendo Four strangers gathered in a group seats swung around facing to play poker and a guy who lives on a mountain with waist-length ponytail jeans tucked into painted fringed leather boots discusses Dorrigo steam trains Big Chief Sitting Bull says the woman in front of me whose husband is used to this used to drive old steam engines we agree they'd be faster than this One passenger called back to Newcastle where the fridges in his sandwich shop have broken down and now the broken-down freight train hemming him in Not his day And the art student in throw it in the washing machine crimplene that flared skinny-topped seventies' image returned to haunt us and our thickening torsos and the small bird woman peak-nosed comb marks in her thick hair feathers growing low on a narrow forehead Three long hours later passengers taking in air sun and nicotine between carriages are asked to close the doors as we rev into motion return of their own accord to correct seat allocations Strangers again we chug slowly past the Dungog picture theatre its cement-rendered facade giving way to a trackside view worn faces reflected in time-worried weatherboards

CONNECTIONS

On the long train to the north coast
a small child screams for stillness
in her hushing mother's arms
The young father sits on the outside
without skills or connection
in flannelette shirt low wool hat
his black olive eyes
a mirror image of his daughter's

On Board Personnel
request that passengers alighting be ready
to do so shortly and that smokers should not
Towards the end of the trip restrictions tighten
warnings are firmer and smokers are smarter
anticipating station pauses are quick on their feet
huddle at open doors in tight knit groups
community resolve strengthening puff by puff
By journey's end they will be firm friends
exchange e-mail addresses and sure enough
our smoker in front forms a book club
returns to her seat with smoker-reader in tow
discusses characterisation in a sci-fi novel

The young father finally moves across
sits beside his small unsettled family
I battle through smokers braving open
carriage doors while the train is moving
As I open the toilet door one smoker
does a slow motion roll backwards
then steadies finds his balance
says he thought he was falling out
of the train everybody's amused
It's no joke I'm told by a railway worker
there are wreaths laid all along the tracks
It seems the warning
on cigarette packets is true
smoking is a danger

Look at You

Look at you
Let me photograph you
close you in my shutter
fold you in my lens
this last moment of you
you and you
and we together
and you again
and over here
and now over there

Look at them
They snap each other
she by the florist
he on a mozaic carpet
of geese and fish
a farmyard of public art
he does not see
only she by the shop window
the plumes of artificial colour
emblematic of their visit

Look at her

how she cries in his arms

strokes his cheek

Look at him

how quietly he weeps

his large youngman lips

loose between tears

Look away

as they sit spread-eagled

on the airport floor

blue carpet whisking

one afar

Look at you

Let me photograph you

before you melt away

distant as forever

Story Bag

with thanks to Kathy, Robbie and Sandra

Talk to a woman about her bag
and she will tell you a story

Somewhere around the Suez Canal where the soft toys are stuffed with disease and bandages I buy a hard leather bag with rough shoulder strap and Egyptian designs In the pocket I keep a 1950 penny (my birth year) only for luck not realising it is also a symbol of my story I keep the bag for a long time but eventually grow out of adolescence and common souvenirs (on the migrant hostel every girl has one) If I still had this bag it would tell stories of things I never thought I would see with my own eyes Topaz seas small wooden boats laden with produce Men with black skin and turbans throwing ropes over the side of the ship and scurrying up them before we'd even docked Colour and bustle belonging to the merchants of history books and foreign empires By the time the ship was in and the gang planks out the market was already in full swing on deck Everything imaginable laid out on patterned carpets magic carpets to sweep us ashore where it is rust red desert dry with too much for a thin child to take in

Talk to a woman about her bag
and she will tell you a story

This roomy bag is string looped covers her lap is blue and white with traditional patterning of mountains and a son's love decorated with fringes strands of wool and fibre rolled on the bare thighs of highland women their skirts hitched up A billum like a child's love expands as you fill it is for significant occasions and every day use After another trip away her son brought home a large banksia pod washed along a beach In this too she recognised the intricate textures of love and kinship Africa is woven into a perfect half egg suspended on black thongs punctuated with beads like ball bearings and bits of bone I follow this basket out of the crowd and all around the park until finally I speak to its owner about her indigo memories her desert earth year and my own fleeting visit just tipping the edge of the continent small boys smiling dancing for the visitors for a half-crown and my long necklace string of grey seed beads bought from a woman in the street and the open air cafe bar where everyone was black and welcoming Squirrels in the gardens and after — the benches the public toilets whites no blacks

Full Moon

with thanks to Susan and Sarah

It is the *haathi** bazaar
It is after the November full moon
The elephants arrive with their traders
legs like trunks of banana trees
ears perfect as the half moon
tips of trunks radiant as rose red

It is the morning
Traders' tents ruffle bright in the breeze
Mahouts lead the elephants through the crowds
They bathe in the river
have their foreheads painted tusks polished

It is the day time trading time
Buffalos cows oxen
All the animals come to this market
horses dogs parrots
monkeys and snakes to be charmed
They look for shade
market stalls are makeshift
The pilgrims arrive

---

* elephant

It is Sonepur the site of a holy battle
where the mighty elephant prevailed

❂

It is midsummer moon
A silver sea hot evening air
and ghostly hulks of steel
Even ships have to go
somewhere to die

The men start as boys
live in shanty towns
work in plot allotments
earn a few dollars a day
and a legacy of workplace hazards
toxic environments
isolation from families
third world disease

It is full moon
A giant vessel waits offshore
The next day it will beach
at high speed on a high tide
to be reduced to nuts and bolts
sheets of metal trucked away
huge piles to be sold

everything from ships' saltcellars
and technology to toilet bowls
and tarpaulins

Poor men swill
in unsanitised conditions
buckets of filth
Marine animals swill
in a heavy metal soup
rest in contaminated sea beds

⭘

So this is India
It is all full moons and shining seas
and memories not of my own
but of my friends who are travellers

One brings back photographs
crowded with people
It is not possible she says
to take a photo without
there are so many people
There are so many photos
she has to buy a mahogany cabinet
with many tiny drawers to house them
When I am in crowded places

I remember these seething images
and lines of her poetry
run through my head

Another stays for a long time
brings back stories and silk scarves
She says I know you can buy
Indian scarves here everywhere
but this is all the way from India itself
When I wear this sea coloured scarf
I remember her stories of India
and how much I missed her
when she was gathering them

How Much?

It will give you new language they say and hand me money to explore it the art of it but I already have the language of it I say as I take the money anyway can't you hear it see the sound of it Listen I say listen to my painted images listen to the dipthong glide of the pigment calculate the collocations of the composition I plunge my hands into this language smear titanium white lampblack Outline in violet Words spill out are streams A face appears it is an artist she sits in a deck chair under a window she stares ice blue hear it gong gong gong gong sing it play it her eyes are drums beating out my verses her tongue spins the story of my skies Are you listening to me I hold up my finished words so you can see them in full colour not everyone can do that I say or dream it Do I still fall silent let me near I put my fingers into the artist enter through her cheekbones tap tap flat notes inside her cranium it is a cerebral portrait strum the soft tissues pat out facial muscles piano tune on the back of her teeth slice down to the ribs borrow two play the bones like an old busker I lie behind her my skin rough on coarse canvas my breasts wet on her fresh paint I find her vocal chords with my lips blow air gently through them Now my words are shapes

shades and tones they arrive in all manner of patterns
float like soap bubbles in the air this language is not
so new I have had it all along can you see that now
How much is that worth?

The Keeper

As a child before speech I was the keeper of language
I held the heart of it in a stone under my tongue
It grew warm against the white cool of my milk teeth

In my birth land language was dense
buried in dried blood crowded with history
Its bones were snatched dust

Nouns were handturned clay pots full bellied
their surfaces seduced in adjective
created by rough hands swinging tureens over
fires that burned in every crack of a sentence

In this land language is spread thin
humming low over prodigious tracts
skimming the surface of tributaries
In the outland of war words are wreaths
of flame and dung hair

The object of language lies in layers of stone
it is the stinging sea it recedes word by word

Words are like stone grown old with meaning
A world without words is a sea frozen over
Trawling for words you will find only
fleets of grinding grumbling oldwife fish

In the soft fall of words that feathers my cloak
pebbles abide wafered claystone grey-dull pitchstone
bloodstone schist and scree strung with staves thin
strokes of ogham script brittle beads of amber black jet
They are beginnings of poems greater than all of us

They await the smooth stone
the heart of language

❂

The poet is a scrag
Coconut hair is stitched
into the wound of her words
She is a pyramid of mouths
they speak in unison
Her eyes are lacerations
her fingers snapping worms

The poet's cloak is blinding
Made from gifts of bird magic
it is blue-banded with summer and oceans
It is a field of violas purple as a pulsing storm
ripe as any fruit deep as a violet mountain crevice
It is gullies rushing with clear pluvial water

She raises her cloaked arm
It is a wingspan of spawn words
There is music
The poetry of the people's song
can be heard above the roar of stones
The poet's mouths grow ominous
They object to liturgies knowing
we are on the edge of war

❂

The heartstone is in a room
the room is voice the voice is space
the space is white the white is wall
the wall is word the word is voice

Women swarm across lands and seas
They enter the white room
murmuring with lips feverish from lighting candles
to the wind the wind which has no ear
veined with soil from moulding monuments
the dirt of bawling infants
their jaws grotesque red bloated
from the effort of keeping talk alive

Paper and vellum are beyond words
The women have used them in protest

shaking silenced voices in perpetrators' faces
folding into fragile birds painting legends
and ruby stonesongs to signal governments
and armies to lay down weapons

The women are watching the wall
They chant
The wall soaks up their babble

There is whisper that the heartstone is so called
because of its shape It sails like breath on wings
around the room storing up echoes and rebounds
resonating with the clay particles of the wall
Soon the women are hearing the stone is heart

They have heart They think the stone could be their heart
One by one the women to save the stonesong slash their chests
rip out their sternums lunge into their rib cages pluck out
their throbbing hearts One by one the women fall

The floor by the snow white wall is red meat
Black crows throng for the startled eyes

The flint edged sky spears the horizon
The earth hesitates
The core rumbles with rumour and riptide

Its mantle broils its crust splits
spews a soup-spill of pulverised narration

Marbled smears will emerge in the stinking wake
of turbulence Latitudes shift
Light drops in cones Strange clans form

❂

I am carnivore
My mouths are insatiable apertures
glistening moist for meat and myth
salivating at the sight of a choice cut
When it becomes story I spit and lick
I tongue at the scent of human morsel

I am greedy for the marrow of corpulent poets
whose words make my mouths water
I exude fire to light their way

❂

Clouds dark as charcoal and menace
roil the skies on self-perpetuating power
A roadtrain veers on two wheels
Everywhere there is derision disparagement
Paradigms fracture actualities fragment

The poet is a composite

of sneers and scuttling scowls

The mouths are chasms

underwater creatures rush in

crustaceans with missiles in their claws

She is a mountain of baby brogues and bodies

A torrent parts the edifice

coffins hoop through this schism

There is a blaze a conflagration

Fissures appear in fields of striated text

New writers cleave to fire-broken rock

The poet's voice is hot lava

roping a spreading karst landscape

It is volcanic spikes needles of crystal

It is spessartine and silver wire

The poet sighs draws silk curtains

like waterfalls to one side of her talk

✪

Visitors arrive at the white room of voice

to see euphony and to taste heartmeat

They hope to take away poems memorable phrases

If they are providential they will glimpse the song

The women's bodies are black mounds
Black blankets cover the floor
the edges crimson rugged
They don't see that carpets bleed

The wall is white light The visitors ignore it
It is many thousands of white paper sheets

The windows are grey rag canvas
They are bold line and vibrant form
in the image of women woman's place
They are stone slabs and lamentation

They are hung high untouchable although executed
by many hands the pigment applied over years
with thick bristle brushes with the hair of pigs
slight trowels the sharp edge of knives razors borers

There are stone celts bronze daggers Hafted adze sickle
and billhook they are the hammer punch and graver pressing
stamping metal They are the chevron borders saltire motifs
The tools are in large amphoras Vessels oozing with colour

The visitors are implored to leave the white
to navigate the black mounds mounds of mud-black night

They are plutocrats compelled to kill the voice of the people
They are magnates in army fatigues and camouflage attire
They avert incriminations allegations of larceny and looting

In the vicinity of the tools the visitors take stealthy steps
reach forward swiftly seize the gem encrusted handles
There is the stench of scorching flesh It is their own
They reel The burnt hands and gouged eyes
of the visitors hurtle from the room

The instruments are the sternums of the women
the women who went before to give their hearts
Their breastbones are the spearheads the swords
defined with gold-leaf and celestial veracity

The dark mounds tremble and rise from the floor
They are silent vestiges in black blanket shrouds
They are the black blanket women

> The poet inclines her head
> Her cloak is vulture wings

I am eagle I am peacock with turquoise auricular feather
I offer my voice to the sun My face is a halo of sty-rimmed eyes
I am fishscales and long speaking hands

Fingers will splice the sky
tears turn to ink
black rains seep into your pores

The mouths are losing patience
They speak in tongues
The poet is fluent in their languages
Her palm is a frond sliding
on the thin stem of her throat
She feels the vibrations of their loquacity
like a sightless person seeking rhythm

The people's confusion is thunderous
They turn away hands over ears
They are deafened they are blinded
their heads have become kessars
sliced skulls with hide stretched taut
The clamorous drumming is within

They sprout horns
From without is archaic string music
They make both death noise and sweet prosody
They pluck syllables from harps lutes lyres

The hills are lambeg drums
summoning gods and marching feet
It is the black blanket women

❂

In the marketplace the stalls overflow

There is a deluge of scarlet rice and macheted limbs

Reporters are counting the slaughtered

X number of slashed throats So many hacked bodies

Meat by the sackful selling by the pound

Young meat infirm meat female meat

embryonic meat from fresh kills of mothers

It is indescribable Words escape them

Photographers arrive attempt to capture the image

of capricious words going over the wall going underground

transmuting as they lizard-scurry under dim doorways

When the words are heard from again they have become

economy indicators money market figures gold and platinum

prices cash rates and currency ceilings parliamentary scams

There are no words for the countless murdered raped

Words are blood-blemished caskets draped in night

Candles burn for them

❂

The black blanket women carry all things white

Their arms are loaves of bread They fly on dove wings

They strip the sticky gags from girl mouths

strap the splits in their wrists break their slave chains

They strip strap pleat new skin

on old whole skin on torn

They collect the scorned mouths

the mutilated lips the severed tongues

They stitch them with cuttyhank and langue

They are bursting flowers goldstone and tiger-eye

pellucid pebbles for my cloak They are river red

The women follow the red river into the marketplace

to the top of government parapets to police blockades

into military mayhem where lives are bought and sold

borders re-routed on a whim or to the chime of coins

Power trades that build empires palaces that sanction

disunite starve The language in these places is money

A red woman rallies the black blanket women on

Her sleeves are water currents They swim in her blood

> The poet is toying
>
> with a medley of nuance and idiom
>
> She is cloaked in rhapsody
>
> Her voice is leaves on a glass roof

What way does the wind blow for you
What part of the wind do you find yourselves in
In the heart quivering
On the outer edge vacillating
In the eye circling
The wind defies speech

The wind lets loose of them and they wheel
A ragged arc of paper disintegrating without voice

⭘

The women make flags from black sticks
and white shards of moon They are waiting

Older women quietly move on the fringes
bucketing red river blood from the streets
They dip their hands into tin pails press them
on the moon-flags Red hands on white moons

The women are ready
In their right hands are the moon-flags
In their left hands they carry bells
In their hearts is the song

The ringing of the bells is red silk linking
them arm to arm foot to softly stepping foot

They advance they dance squat
give birth to smooth round moonstones

> The poet walks shadowly
> in the background of her vision
> Calmly she lifts off the pyramid of mouths
> approaches the red woman
> positions the writhing mass on her brow
> like a crown
> It is the blood of all the women
> the milk of all the mothers
> the fortitudes of the spirits of terra
> the lyrics of the song
>
> The poet is careworn her voice timeworn
> Without the mouths she is an empty room

✿

There is a place within where I go to lie
It is soft as a nest fashioned from twigs and down
a safe inscape where no one else cares dares enter

In this otherworld leaves drip with the dappled magic
of lore It is dry as tinder while all around in earthlands
there is precipitation In those moments between warm
hearths and cheerlessness remember me

Bring me words heavy with spirit Bring me bread
Bring me the crumbs of pristine poems

⚬

The poet's cloak is batholithic
its shoulders are a plateau its sleeves
basalt columns the pebbles are granite tors
they hold the precision of higher poems

The poet stoops under the weight of poetry and stone
The earth quakes as she returns to the lake country
its translucent pools and succulent
shoreside growth splintered with beige sands
rippled black fertility

Painstakenly she removes the cloak rests it
on the foreshore The ground pulsates

She wears a collar of gold to illuminate her journey
her *crannog** obscured by straw mist and languorous
deliberation Slowly she peels away slim ribbons of
syntax purls them between forefinger and thumb

She beads white notes
with yellow membrane and madder root

---

* lake dwelling

The pellets multiply collect at her feet like lapilli
a water-worn breeze teases her into pure phrase
She is scant ribs and pock belly

She is not yet free
She drags on mulberry memory
hauls it from her gut unwinds her whole being

She is a multicoloured *crios** woven over
many seasons She is a stream of story
Insular inscription lead tablets
drowned in the springs of deities

She strips words from the sweep of sash
gathers up the fresh corn seed of her flesh

No one knows what the poet's closing word will be
only that it will have perfect pitch perfect tone

---

* belt

The people are restless

They fear her power may be reduced to loam

From under her tongue she rolls a solitary dazzling

jewel adds it to the feast in the hammocked cloak

She summons enough vigor for one fierce flit of it

❂

The earth's rim is a wide wedge of dusk

spangled with milestones symbols of truth

It is a rose wash of allegory and free flowing verse

A child kisses her mother with young words

In the child's pink mouth a warm stone

sings against tiny moons and baby teeth

and I am footprints in water-lapped sand

a fine smile of silt the distant laughing tide

❂

Also by Lizz Murphy

Wee Girls

Women Writing from an Irish Perspective

Lizz Murphy (Ed.)

A moving and often amusing collection of fiction, poetry and autobiography by top-selling and award-winning writers.

Tales of blood and bloodlines — Irish grandmothers, ma's and da's, the Famine and the Troubles. Whatever the form, there are the stories, the music, the whispering dreams and the voices that ache to be heard.

There is a wildness and a daring in these voices. They call up legions out of the sea and set fires alight. They hang out over garden fences, move restlessly, are dotey, beaming, weeping, powerful.

"A remarkable collection."

— Phillip Adams

"A nice big fat value-for-money anthology with an extremely broad range."

— Margie Cronin, *Refractory Girl*

ISBN 1 875559 51 5

Poems from the Madhouse
Sandy Jeffs

This is disturbing but quite wonderful poetry, because of its clarity, its humour, its imagery, and the insights it gives us into being human, being mad, being sane. I read and read—and was profoundly moved. I delighted in it as poetry; I was touched by its honesty, courage and vulnerability.

— Anne Deveson

The language challenges her with fifty names for madness, writing of a life of vigilance and struggle, she enlarges our understanding of human capacity.

— Judith Rodriguez

Certificate of Commendation, Human Rights Award for Poetry, 1994
Second Prize, Anne Elder FAW Award, 1994

ISBN 1 876756 03 9

Blood Relations

Sandy Jeffs

Bearing witness was unbearable.

— Sandy Jeffs

Sandy Jeff's poems inhabit the darkness at the heart of the dysfunctional family. The ravaged emotionality of these poems will speak to anyone who has felt its pain.

— Doris Brett

... a courageous and powerful journey . . . Sandy Jeffs explores the dynamics including the secrecy, the unspeakable effects on the children, and the healing.

— Patricia Easteal

These poems speak with confronting directness of family lives deeply scarred by love distorted, by raging violence, alcohol, madness. It is as if only a language 'scoured' of artifice and sentimentality can encompass such experiences of Blood Relations, *and chart the complex and fluctuating reactions of bewilderment, anger, guilt and compassion that mark indelibly these memoirs of a survivor.*

— Jennifer Strauss

ISBN 1 875559 98 1

Bird

Susan Hawthorne

Many-eyed and many-lived is this poet, as seismologist or lover, bird or newborn child. To the classic figures of Sappho or Eurydice she brings all the Now! Here! sense of discovery that fires her modern girl taking lessons in flight.

— Judith Rodriguez

ISBN 1 875559 88 4

Wire Dancing

Patricia Sykes

In poems that are at once allusive and elusive, Sykes leaps like an acrobat between past and present, mythology and history, the everyday and the exotic, from Bosnia to the circus. And, dancing nimbly along the high wires of emotion and intellect, she is passionate, witty, erudite and ironic . . . the poetry experience of the year.

— Bev Roberts

Commended, Anne Elder FAW Award, 2000
Commended, Mary Gilmore Award, 2000

ISBN 1 875559 90 6

St Suniti and the Dragon

Suniti Namjoshi

An original imagination full of surprises from Beowulf to Bangladesh.

I can think of plenty of adjectives to describe St Suniti and the Dragon, *but not a noun to go with them. It's hilarious, witty, elegantly written, hugely inventive, fantastic, energetic . . . With work as original as this, it's easier to fling words at it than to say what it is or what it does.*

— U. A. Fanthorpe

ISBN 1 875559 18 3

Feminist Fables

Suniti Namjoshi

An ingenious reworking of fairy tales from East and West. Mythology, mixed with the author's original material and vivid imagination. An indispensable feminist classic.

Her imagination soars to breathtaking heights ... she has the enviable skill of writing stories that are as entertaining as they are thought-provoking.

— Kerry Lyon, *Australian Book Review*

ISBN 1 875559 19 1

The Body in Time
Diane Fahey

Diane Fahey pieces together a world — with integrity and incomparable delicacy — much as the fragile light of a star defines a universe.

— Annie Greet

Nervous Arcs
Jordie Albiston

Jordie Albiston writes with a sharp intelligence, lyrical grace, and moral passion. A name to watch for.

— Janette Turner

Winner, Mary Gilmore Award, 1996
Second Prize, Anne Elder FAW Award, 1996

ISBN 1 875559 37 X

Summer was a Fast Train without Terminals

Merlinda Bobis

An epic of the old Philippines, lyrical reflections on longing, and an erotic dance drama are included in this fine collection.

Bobis can produce some genuinely haunting pieces. This is a touching work from an established poet.

— Hamesh Wyatt

Shortlisted *Age* Book of the Year, 1998

ISBN 81 875559 76 0

If you would like to know more about Spinifex Press,

write for a free catalogue or visit our home page.

SPINIFEX PRESS

PO Box 212, North Melbourne,

Victoria 3051, Australia

www.spinifexpress.com.au